WALT DISNEP'S
PONGO and PERDY
Two Happy Dalmatians

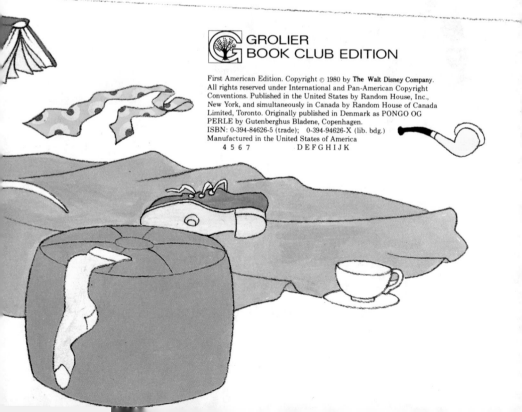

GROLIER
BOOK CLUB EDITION

First American Edition. Copyright © 1980 by The Walt Disney Company.
All rights reserved under International and Pan-American Copyright
Conventions. Published in the United States by Random House, Inc.,
New York, and simultaneously in Canada by Random House of Canada
Limited, Toronto. Originally published in Denmark as PONGO OG
PERLE by Gutenberghus Bladene, Copenhagen.
ISBN: 0-394-84626-5 (trade); 0-394-94626-X (lib. bdg.)
Manufactured in the United States of America
      4 5 6 7   D E F G H I J K

I am Pongo, the Dalmatian.
I want to tell you about my family.
But first, I will tell you about Roger.

I live with Roger.
We have a lovely home.
But Roger is busy writing songs.
He does not spend much time with me.
And he forgets to do things.

He forgets to wash the dishes.

He forgets to put
his clothes away.

One day he forgot to give me water.

I decided Roger
needed someone
to keep him
company.
   He needed a wife
to sing his
songs to!
   I started to
look for one.

I saw many nice
ladies.

I saw a lady artist
with a long skinny
hound.

I saw a French lady
with a poodle.

I saw a chubby
lady eating an
ice-cream cone.

She had a chubby dog.

Not one was right
for my owner, Roger.

Then I saw the perfect lady!
And she was walking with a
beautiful Dalmatian.

But it was only four-thirty.

Roger does not take me to the park until five o'clock.

If we did not hurry, we would miss the perfect lady.

I decided to move the hands on the clock.

Then I brought Roger his hat.

"Pongo, old boy,"
said Roger. "Is it
five o'clock already?
I almost forgot about
your walk."

That was just
what I wanted
Roger to say!

I pulled and tugged on the leash with all my might.

We had to get to the park quickly.

Roger held my leash tightly.

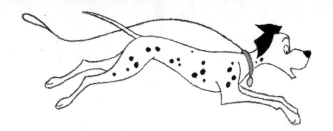

Finally I broke away
from Roger.

I ran through the park
as fast as I could.

I saw the lady
artist painting a
picture of her dog.

Then I saw the
chubby lady eating
a sandwich.

Her chubby dog
was eating, too.

I saw the French
lady taking a drink
of water.

Her poodle
sat nearby.

I was about to give up hope.
Then I saw the perfect lady!
She was sitting on a bench.
She was reading a book.
Next to her sat her pretty Dalmatian.
But what was I to do?

I looked for Roger.

Then I had a great idea!

Roger was sitting and writing a song.
I ran up behind him.
I grabbed his hat.

"Stop, Pongo! Stop!" Roger shouted.
"Bring my hat back right now!"

He did just what I had wanted him to do.

I carried his hat to the park bench.

And he followed me.

I put the hat down right next to the
perfect lady.

"Excuse me, Miss," Roger said politely.
"But Pongo was playing with my hat."
Hmm... a good start, I said to myself.

"That's all right," the perfect lady said.
"My Perdy plays like that too, sometimes."
Perdy, I said to myself. What a lovely
name!
And for me and Perdy, it was love
at first sight.

Then Roger spoiled everything.
He turned to leave!
I could not let him go away.
I sat down and did not move.
I barked and barked.
I ran around Roger and the lady.
Perdy barked and ran around
them, too.

In a few minutes, two leashes, two dogs,
and two people were all tangled together!!

SPLASH!
We all fell into the pond!

But we all came up laughing!
"My name is Roger," said my owner.
"And I am Anita," said the perfect lady.
"Let's have a cup of coffee," said Roger.

The park was lovely that evening.
We walked and talked in the moonlight.
Roger liked Anita.
Anita liked Roger.
That made Perdy and me happy.

A few months later, Roger and Anita
were married!

Perdy and I waited for them outside
the chapel.

But that is not the end of the story...

Anita and Perdy came to live at our house.
Nanny came to live at our house, too.
Nanny washed the dishes and served
the coffee.
And Nanny was kind
to everyone.

Nanny cooked meals for Roger and Anita.
She also made sure that Perdy and I had
good food and fresh water.

Every day!

A few months later, Perdy said,
"Pongo, I have good news for you.
We are going to have a family."
"A family?" I asked.

"Puppies!" Anita told Roger. " Perdy
is going to have puppies!"

All of us could hardly wait.

Finally the big day arrived.
It was time for the puppies to be born.
Anita gave Perdy a cozy basket.
"Perdy, dear," said Anita, "I will stay
with you the whole time."

Roger and I waited in the living room.
Nanny ran back and forth to the kitchen.
She carried bowls of warm water.

Roger and I waited for hours.
We paced back and forth.
Then Nanny peeked in.
She held up five fingers.
"Perdy has had five puppies,"
she said. "And there are more
on the way!"

Soon Nanny peeked in again.
Now she held up ten fingers.
"Congratulations," she said.
"Pongo, you are the father
of ten beautiful Dalmatian
puppies!"

"Hooray!" shouted Roger.
"Yip, yip, yippy!"
I barked.

But our joy did not last.
Anita came into the room.
"I'm sorry, Pongo," she said.
"One of the puppies is not moving."

"Poor little puppy," said Roger sadly.
Roger laid the bundle down.
I gave it a nudge with my nose...

and the bundle moved!

A little nose popped out of
the blanket.

I wagged my tail happily.

"He's alive!" said Anita.
I barked for joy.
I knew how happy Perdy would be.
I thought we should name this
puppy Lucky.

The puppies stayed in their basket
for two weeks.
Then they climbed out.
They began to look around.
Roger and Anita always counted them.

It would be easy for
one to get lost.
And they loved the
puppies too much to
lose one.

Perdy was a very good mother.
She was always watching the puppies.
We enjoyed our family.

Soon the puppies got big.
They were big enough to walk
in the park.
Lucky was a little slow.
It did not matter.
We loved him very much.
We loved all our puppies very much.

And that is the end of my story.
We all still live happily together.